SHORT CUTS

Alan Blackwood likes to call the fifty little pieces in this collection 'vignettes'. They are certainly not conventional short stories, but situations and images observed and described with the greatest economy of words. Less is more has been his motto while writing them, and in the process he has created what is perhaps a new literary genre.

SHORT CUTS

Alan Blackwood

ARTHUR H. STOCKWELL LTD
Torrs Park   Ilfracombe   Devon
Established 1898
www.ahstockwell.co.uk

British Library Cataloguing-in-Publication Data.
A catalogue record for this book is available
from the British Library.

These are entirely fictional stories,
and no conscious attempt has been made
to accurately record or recreate
any real-life events.

By the same author:
Writer's Cramp

ISBN 978-0-7223-4101-8
Printed in Great Britain by
Arthur H. Stockwell Ltd
Torrs Park   Ilfracombe
Devon

BIOGRAPHICAL DETAILS

Alan Blackwood is the author of numerous books on music, including a biography of the famous conductor Sir Thomas Beecham. More recently he has turned to fiction. Several of the pieces in this collection have been published in various magazines, and he is currently working on a revision of his first novel.

CONTENTS

TWO'S COMPANY

Nice things only happen when you're looking the other way.

'May I?' She indicated the seat across the table and tucked herself in with a little silken kiss of her legs. She smiled and raised her glass, rattling her bangles. 'Cheers!'

We began to roll with the open sea, and through the window a necklace of lights was strung along the coast.

'Brighton's my home town,' I said. 'Well, Hove actually, but Brighton has more of a ring to it.'

She eyed me over the rim of her glass. 'Are you a writer or something?'

'I've had one or two books published. Nothing fancy.'

'It must be wonderful to write.' She watched the lights of the ferry going the other way. 'Ships that pass in the night,' she added dreamily. 'I love going places, don't you?'

'Not at night,' I said. The water and the darkness were like crossing the river Lethe. You felt your memory and identity being washed away.

The mascara, the eyelashes, gave her the wide-eyed stare of a doll. Who was she, all on her own, on this ship, in the middle of the night?

A distant beam of light swung in a lazy arc. The French coast.

'Hasn't the time gone quickly!' She looked at her watch and smiled again, over my shoulder. 'All right, darling?'

Bill had to take his pill and go and lie down as soon as they got on board.

'Are you okay?' She glanced at what was left of my bottle of duty free.

Down on the car deck I saw them again, with two stickers over their windscreen, Bill and Sandra. Then we were off, like bats out of hell.

Ships that pass in the night. And hangovers that don't.

* * * * *

DELHI BELLY

'Monsoon?' Geraldine snapped. 'Rubbish!'

Sorry I spoke, but I'd never heard rain like it. You could hardly think to play Scrabble. I put down otiose. She wasn't having that either. 'That's not a word!'

Geraldine had been on at me for ages to join her on one of her trips, buying batiks, gems and jewellery for her boutique. We'd stay with Florrie, she had so many friends out there, and everything was so cheap. We'd have such fun.

She won the Scrabble and wanted a drink, with ice of course. Florrie never took ice in her gin, and I doubt if she knew where those cubes in the freezer had come from or how long they'd been in there. Make that Scotch on the rocks for one.

'I'll swear it's nothing I gave you,' Florrie said, as we watched the ambulance drive away.

She lit a new cigarette from the stub of the old, the last gasp of the Raj. 'Poor lassie. A lonely wee soul. She was so pleased to have you here.'

Florrie clapped her hands at a fat old crow perched on the window ledge. 'They help to keep down the cockroaches,' she said. This one flapped his wings and dipped out of sight, a bellyful of cockroach.

The aircraft dipped a wing over the fuzz of lights below. Lying on your bed down there, listening to the hum and whirr of the fan, waiting for the next faint gust of air, till someone got up from their bed rather fast and started making dreadful noises in the bathroom, where things always sounded worse.

'Drink sir?' They were soon round with the trolley.

A whisky and soda perhaps.

'Ice?'

'No thanks.'

* * * * *

BUNNY CLUB

At Earl's Court she got on the train and I knew her at once. The bunny teeth, just touching the lower lip, to produce an expression of – how could I put it – glum content. Homely was the unhappy word.

The dating agency had sent me her name and phone number. Her voice hadn't sounded too bad over the phone, and we arranged to meet by the bookstall at Holborn Station. She'd be wearing a lucky rabbit's foot.

The half stab of arousal, riding the escalator up towards the arc of light at the top. The press of people, parting briefly to reveal a figure by the bookstall, with a lucky rabbit's foot in the lapel of her coat and that homely look.

A second's hesitation, why waste each other's time, and back down the other escalator, back along the labyrinthine passageways, back into the next crowded train, back into the tunnel, the gut of the great big city, the peristaltic wobble of wires and pipes along the tunnel wall, and one lump of shit on the move.

Green Park. Suzie got up to go. Suzie Rose. They didn't show too much, those teeth. But if it hadn't been them it would have been something else, thick ankles, flat tits, big hips. It didn't take much to hand you a short straw in the genetic lottery of life.

I caught her eye as she moved towards the doors. Not a flicker. Of course not, you bastard. How long, I wonder, did she wait by the bookstall, all of twenty years ago?

Stand clear of the closing doors. Bye bye Suzie, for a second time. Forgive me if you can.

* * * * *

BLUE NOTE

'All right,' Henry replied to Harriet's request. 'If you twist my arm.'

I'd like to see her try. Henry was built like a boxer, though he didn't play Brahms and Liszt with the gloves on. He was a heavyweight of the keyboard, and a useful guest at Harriet's dinner parties.

He now padded obediently across the room to the waiting baby grand, stretched his fingers, then sank them into one of Brahms' late piano pieces. No thunderous chords or cascading arpeggios this time. The notes fell like autumn raindrops, as Harriet served coffee and passed round the chocolate mints.

'Lovely,' we murmured at the end of it. 'Great stuff Henry!' I added, perhaps a little high on the sherry trifle. 'Now how about some Blues!'

After one of his occasional town hall recitals I'd joined him up on the platform and we'd played around with Bad Penny Blues, till the caretaker chucked us out.

Henry's mouth softened into a smile. His eyes lit up beneath the bushy brows. They met Harriet's stony gaze.

'Thank you Henry.' She looked pointedly at her watch. 'We mustn't let you miss your train.'

I drove him back to the station. 'Still teaching?' I asked. He had an upright piano in his upstairs flat for that.

'Any more recitals coming up?' Apparently not. His agent had dropped him. A scholarship to the Royal College of Music and winner of two piano competitions were not enough.

'Anyway, see you next time,' I said, as with difficulty Henry eased himself out of my little car.

'If there is one.' He unfolded his plastic mac to the first real spots of rain.

* * * * *

HONEY MOON

Susan took a sip from my glass and rolled the cloudy liquid round her tongue. 'Liquorice?' she inquired of the taste.

It was, I told her, aniseed in pastis. In the old days it would have been absinthe. There was a painting by Degas called Absinthe, of a man and a woman seated outside a café with a glass of it between them, looking thoroughly fed up and with nothing left to say. Marriage might have been a better title.

Susan's big brother Geoff had just got married, and we were celebrating at this charming little bistro, with chairs and tables set out on the pavement in the warm, purple dusk.

'And is there honey still for tea!' Geoff quoted gleefully, as the waiter poured some over his pudding.

A man at the next table turned sharply round, old school tie, clipped moustache, the lot, the cartoon Englishman abroad.

'Did I hear somebody say honey?' He had the voice as well.

His wife, it had to be, tugged miserably at his sleeve. He shook her off.

'Arthur's the name. I'll tell you something about honey. Bees actually. Knew this beekeeper chap. Got a bit careless. One day the queen settled on him and the whole swarm followed.' Arthur wagged a finger. 'Poor bugger wasn't stung. Not once. Suffocated to death.'

Geoff's bride, a shrinking violet up till now, smacked a hand to her mouth then returned her share of everything.

'My bloody jacket!' Arthur toppled off his chair. 'My bloody tie!'

'Better out than in,' Susan whispered, giggled and squeezed my hand.

Very nice. Just watch it, that's all.

* * * * *

OPEN WIDE

They say you can't smell vodka on the breath. But I don't think the dentist was deceived, and he wasn't taking any chances. It was just two quick jabs in the gum before he started digging out Lisa's deeply impacted molar, piece by tiny piece. It sounded bad enough from the waiting room.

The trouble was that without those three stiff drinks and the tranquillisers, we'd never have got her out of the house and into my car for the appointment.

I used to commission from Lisa illustrations for children's books. She had real talent and made a good living till the agoraphobia kicked in and the work dried up.

What dark malaise of mind or soul lay behind her fear of open spaces? And what was it like, year in year out, sitting all day beneath that faded piece of artwork for Cinderella, with the vodka and the pills, terrified to feel the fresh air and the sun upon her face?

Nothing else wanted to leave home either, the old mops and brushes in the bath (did she ever take one?), the leftovers in the kitchen, the broken armchair, the threadbare carpets, the withered plants, the dust and grime that made you cough and sneeze and start to itch.

'I want a drink!' Lisa mumbled, back in the house and holding an antiseptic pad to her butchered jaw.

'You'll have to wait!' Tom shouted back. I don't know what his problem was but he hadn't worked in years either. They needed each other to yell at.

Anyway, I'd done my bit. I stepped over bundles of old newspapers in the bare hallway.

'Thanks a lot.' Tom saw me out. 'Take care.'

With that nasty crack in the lintel over the front door, he could say that again.

* * * * *

DOG'S DINNER

Yappy Popeyes was a chihuahua, a breed of dog from Mexico, and one of those famous hats would have snuffed him out. You could hold him in one hand, though I wouldn't have advised it. He crapped and snapped at the same time. A nice trick, if you can do it.

It wouldn't have surprised me either if Pat breast fed Yappy Popeyes, the way she hugged him to her bosom.

'Poor darling,' she said. 'It's the heat.' He'd just thrown up.

Pat and Mike had a holiday home in my village and they'd had me round for drinks. But I wasn't having Yappy Popeyes back in my house, with all his tricks. So I was taking them to see my friend Louise. She had a lovely garden and liked animals.

'Quel mignon!' Louise said politely. 'But is it not a problem, coming all the way down here with the little dog?'

Ask Mike. The vaccination certificates, the pills and powders, the long drive to the coast, the Channel crossing, the longer, hotter drive the other side, the mopping up.

'He's as good as gold!' Pat replied stoutly, just as Yappy Popeyes began to emit a half-strangled wail. Louise's old cat had ambled into the garden looking for a spot of shade.

Pat clutched Yappy Popeyes even closer to her bosom. 'Can you get rid of that cat!'

Never mind her. Goliath had broken loose again. God knows what sort of a dog he was, but he now thundered through the garden door, all shaggy hair and dribble, knocking over the drinks table, and Pat off her chair.

Yappy Popeyes performed a somersault in the air. Another trick, and his last.

Thank you, Goliath.

* * * * *

DOUBLE TROUBLE

As if Christmas and the New Year weren't bad enough, there was Halloween. Look at them, prancing about in their black pointed cardboard hats, faces daubed white or painted a dyspeptic green, and half their teeth blacked out. Adults, they called themselves.

Those few of us who were above such antics, or who couldn't be bothered, stuck together and spoke of more important things.

'Doppelgängers!' Freda boomed, a big girl with a taste in shawls and beads, who read palms and the tarot cards.

'A German word,' she informed us, 'meaning your double, your other self. To see your Doppelgänger is an omen of death.'

The chime on Bruce's mobile rudely interrupted her. Bruce fancied himself as a ladies' man and a bit of a comedian. He winked at us, pinched his nose, and answered his mobile in a low spooky voice, 'Hello, this is your Doppelgänger speaking.'

Whoever or whatever was calling soon wiped the satisfied grin off his face.

'M-me,' he stuttered, let go of his nose, and swallowed hard. 'At this party. Halloween.'

Bruce flopped into a chair, the mobile still pressed to his ear, and he began to sweat. He stared at his rolled-gold watch. 'In about half an hour,' he said and called off.

The long, lank strands of hair he combed so assiduously over his pate fell about his ears. The medallion he wore on a chain under his half-open shirt dangled like a plumb line.

'The missus.' Bruce looked helplessly up at us. 'She's come back.'

An omen of death as near as dammit.

* * * * *

FLEA MARKET

'Got to go back to Blighty for a week or two,' Bunty announced from inside her tweeds.

She'd bought the old house in the village that had been empty for as long as anyone could remember. Some of the older folk crossed themselves as they passed by.

'See what's in the room at the back.' Bunty handed me a bunch of keys on an iron ring fit for the Bastille.

Generations of woodworm had broken their teeth on the door to that room. I nearly broke a collar bone trying to open it. As for the smell inside, let's say I'd have been a fool to strike a match.

Grey hammocks of cobweb hung across one small window. Fallen rafters had turned to mouldy dust. Floorboards looked ready to give me the drop into an oubliette. And in the dim half light I made out a white marble slab propped against the blackened fireplace.

'That room's full of fleas or something,' I reported back to Bunty. I showed her the angry bites on my hands and wrists. 'And there's a marble plaque in the fireplace.'

'Marble plaque?' Bunty snapped. A retired headmistress, she was used to asking questions.

'Yes, the kind you see in cemeteries. It's got some lettering on it.'

Bunty began to polish her glasses. 'What's it doing there?'

'Christ knows, but I'd take a closer look at that fireplace, if I were you.' I scratched at a bite. 'Just in case.'

'In case of what?' Tiny beads of sweat adhered to the soft fur on Bunty's upper lip. 'I'd do something about those bites, if I were you.'

* * * * *

BLUE EYES

Mr Smoky is a real fat cat, with a coat of grey fur as thick as a Persian rug. When he sees me coming down the street he rolls over on his back, a sure sign of trust. He's everybody's friend. Not like Blue Eyes. She didn't want to know, just turned away and took refuge under the nearest parked car, or retreated into the garden of that empty house down the road. Always hanging about round there, as though it was her home.

In fact, jungle was a better name for that garden. An object lesson in the force of nature to take over at the drop of a hat. Peer long enough into that riot of unchecked growth and you might see one of the painter Henri Rousseau's fabulous tigers staring back at you, unless it was Blue Eyes herself. They were the largest things about her, like the eyes of a hungry child.

That was before they started clearing up. No more Blue Eyes, you might think. But there she was, as they hacked and chopped away, sitting by the front door of the house, cleaning her paws in the sun, as though she owned the place. Things are looking up, she seemed to say.

Now it's flowers again in the garden and curtains in the windows of the house. But it's not Blue Eyes who sits on the welcome mat by the new front door. The coat looks familiar, but that mog is better groomed than Blue Eyes could ever hope to be.

Still, she was happy for a week or two, which is as good as it gets for most of us, unless we're a real fat cat.

* * * * *

DEAD END

Jane and I loved old cemeteries, crumbling ruins, sombre evergreens, the whole theatre of melancholy and decay, and I thought I knew somewhere that had it all.

On school holidays I used to stay with my grandmother in her sleepy old market town, set in a watercolour world, a place of gas lamps, alleyways, secrets and shadows.

I loved the sunken path through the Castle grounds that came out by the town cemetery where the air was dark with the call of rooks.

Best of all was the walk over the bridge, across the water meadows and down a line of horse chestnut trees, to the deserted chapel. Its little domed tower just reached above thickets of those sombre evergreens and a tangle of undergrowth. Tombs and headstones wallowed like shipwrecks, fallen plaster littered pews and flagstones, fingers of creeper poked through broken lattice window panes. To stand in there, scratched and torn, in the dim half light, listening to the beat of my heart, was to share its sad and silent rapture.

Now Jane was going to share it too.

First we had to find somewhere to park in granny's not so sleepy old town. I hardly recognised the place. But the bridge was much as I remembered it, and the river that still slipped placidly beneath its arches. And to my joy, on the far river bank, there was the stile I'd clambered over so many times as a lad, at the start of the walk across the water meadows.

I grabbed Jane's hand and whispered, 'Nearly there!'

Private property said the notice on the gate, where the horse chestnut trees used to be.

Never go back, they say. But who ever listens to good advice.

* * * * *

BARE FACTS

Madame Butterfly, as I called her, tapped on my door and poked her head round it. She wanted to change the sheets.

'Come in,' I said, lying on top of the bed in my red and white striped pyjamas.

'Okay!' she gasped, and fled.

Time to make a move in any case. Over by the window, down below and across the street, an old black man was slumped on the sidewalk with his back to a wall. He'd collected a few odds and ends, some items of crockery, some dog-eared paperbacks, and a teddy bear, one ear half off, and two large button eyes, wide with appeal. I pulled a sweat shirt over my pyjamas and was down there like a shot.

'He's quite a guy!' the black man chuckled, pocketing my two bucks and handing me the bear. He was too, with a strip of cloth above each eye, unusual for a bear.

Crossing the road again I glanced up Russian Hill where, in the words of the song, little cable cars climb half way to the stars, to give you a grandstand view across the Bay to Alcatraz Island where Al Capone was once a guest.

Now I knew who my new friend was. Eyebrows Alcatraz, the bear that got away.

Back in the hotel elevator, I pressed the button to go up. Madame Butterfly just beat me to it, and we went down to the basement, where she waited with another pile of fresh linen.

'Going up?' I smiled.

'Okay!' She recoiled in horror, leaving me and Eyebrows to ascend, slowly and shakily, half way to the stars, or at least to the second floor.

* * * * *

HALF TIME

It was vandalism to have sliced that old wooden figurehead down the middle, though the half that Lotte had up on her wall, of a buxom wench cresting a wave, did look good.

Lotte crept up behind me and turned down the volume on The Flying Dutchman Overture. 'I need you,' she whispered in my ear.

For her birthday party she'd bought a large fresh fish that flopped over the kitchen sink, too big to go in the oven. She handed me her sharpest kitchen knife. 'Please cut off the head.'

I looked upon the clouded lifeless eye, at the woeful, clown-like droop of the mouth of that poor fish, and couldn't do it.

Lotte turned round from peeling potatoes. 'Mein Gott! I said the head not the bloody tail!' She snatched the knife from me and took two or three frantic swipes to sever head from body. Public executions must often have been like that.

'You are a bloody wimp!' she shouted, rinsing her hands under the tap.

It wasn't her words, it was her face, all twisted down one side with anger and contempt. I slammed her front door behind me, ran over the road to my car and caught my own face in the driving mirror, all twisted down one side.

We joked about our good side and our bad side, but it was true. Jekyll and Hyde cases, all of us.

Across the road a baleful light shone behind Lotte's curtains. Some birthday party. Run back now before it was too late.

With a crunch of gears I raced away, from Lotte, and from half a figurehead with half an enigmatic smile on her face.

* * * * *

CAT FLAP

Wait by the phone and it'll never ring. My internal answerphone buzzed instead. A woman downstairs by the front door asked if she could leave a notice at our block of flats about a missing cat.

There were two of them down there, wrapped up against the cutting east wind under a sky as grey and hard as pumice. Lost, said their notice, above a colour picture of a tortoiseshell kitten, startled perhaps by the flash of the camera. Her name was Biscuit.

'Poor little Biscuit,' I said, taking a copy of the notice, but they'd already gone, too cold and too distressed to hang about. That was the thing about love and anxiety. Those who endured it must often suffer the most.

One good thing, the weather took a turn for the better. The mild west wind returned, bringing a breath of the wide ocean, billowing white clouds, and occasional rain, to trickle down all those other pictures, stuck on fences and round lamp posts, of the same startled little face.

'Any luck?' Coming back from the shops I was sure it was one of those women, now stripped down to plastic mac and ankle-length green wellies.

'Biscuit,' I reminded her. She frowned and hurried on.

If only I'd found Biscuit, bedraggled and half-starved but thankfully still alive. A different story then, for two ladies who might be more than just good friends and a bloke with a thing about ankle-length green wellies.

I switched on the kettle, dropped a tea bag in a mug, and tried not to wait for anything.

* * * * *

LAST WALTZ

At one of Walter's parties I found an old electric keyboard and tried a few bars of Stormy Weather. Next thing, Walter had picked me up on alto sax and the joint was jumping.

On the phone next day, he told me he'd played in a dance band way back in his Brylcreem days and kept all his old sheet music. Night and Day, Blue Skies, Body and Soul, September in the Rain. The years fell away as Walter ran through the list.

'The Christmas party's coming up,' he went on. 'We'll play for that. You saw 'em last night. People love live music. They'll be eating out of our hand!'

Not quite the way he meant. The Christmas buffet was always something special, but Walter couldn't wait. 'Here comes the Chattanooga Choo Choo!' he bellowed into the mike to a shriek of feedback, and off we raced to a clatter of plates, forks and spoons. We soon had to stop again for the raffle.

'Couldn't wait to get rid of us,' Walter almost sobbed, as the thud of the club ghetto blaster pursued us from the church hall back to my car. The tambourine he'd bought, to double on when things got really hot, was never out of its case.

He snatched off his paper hat. 'If that's what they want, they can all get fucking stuffed!'

Such a shame. Come summer we might still have been a hit. Tea for Two, cha cha cha, to the seductive tap and rattle of the tambourine, under the fairy lights of all those trim little gardens from Teddington to Edgware.

That, as Walter had also said, was how to pull the birds. Only in the Playmates club they were mostly old boilers, Beryl, Vera, Olive, stuffed or otherwise.

* * * * *

AVE MARIA

Dora clapped her hands. 'It's as pretty as a picture!'

Café tables and chairs stood in the dappled shade of plane trees. Swifts and swallows dived and wheeled, translating brightest day into little shrieks of joy. Pont Saint Esprit. Bridge of the Holy Spirit.

'Isn't that a lovely name, dear!'

Reg swiped at a fly.

Auntie Dora and Uncle Reg, who used to send me socks for Christmas. I hardly remembered them, but they'd shown up out of the blue, and I'd better take them somewhere.

We parked and Reg pointed to another car. 'Dutch,' he observed with a sniff.

'Take your cap off, Reg,' Dora said, before we entered the abbey church, where the painted columns rose to a vaulted ceiling patterned with stars. She paused by a statue of the Virgin, a halo of more stars raised above the head by a loop of wire.

'D doesn't really stand for Dutch, does it?' Dora whispered with a shy little smile and a squeeze of my hand. 'Reg doesn't say much, but I know he's loving it too.'

Outside again he seemed to be, with his bottle of the local liqueur from the gift shop. He broke the seal and took a healthy swig.

'Think I don't know what D really stands for?' He wiped his mouth with the back of his hand. 'Bloody Jerries!'

He sat in the car with the hiccups and a red nose that was starting to peel. Dora's eyes were rather red as well.

Late afternoon sunlight flooded the rear window, casting a halo about her head, no loop attached.

'It's all so lovely,' she sighed, with that same little smile.

* * * * *

39

CURTAIN CALL

Away from the footlights greasepaint does no one any favours. Julia's face was a shade of nicotine mixed with soot. Lady Bracknell in The Importance of Being Ernest.

Also in the bar after that first night was Peter as an exquisite Algernon Moncrieff, accompanied as always by Jeremy the director, and Tony, in the dog collar and gaiters of Canon Chasuble.

'You're a disgrace to the cloth!' Polly the barmaid gibed as he elbowed his way back to the bar.

Peter giggled. Tony swung round, face red and fists clenched. Jeremy looked for somewhere to put his glass. He played rugby too.

Julia pressed my hand. 'See you by the car park in ten minutes.'

Why was there so much bitchiness, so much frustration, behind the happy curtain calls? Perhaps it was worse among amateurs, who felt they'd missed their true vocation and all the more jealously nursed their dreams and their egos, if not always their livers.

Coming up the path behind me someone tripped and fell into a puddle. I recognised Peter's giggle.

Tony picked himself up. 'Right, you little poofter!'

Jeremy emerged from the shadows.

Julia tugged at her seat belt. 'Let's go.'

Past Hampton Court Palace and over the bridge, we drove into a cosy world of large half-timbered houses, Jaguars and Porsches in the driveways, gentrified pubs, and churches flying the flag of Saint George.

How did it go? Saint George for England! Saint Pancras for Scotland! A good old chestnut for Canon Chasuble in the Tudor Players' Christmas pantomime, if he still had his teeth.

* * * * *

NORTHERN LINE

'To the cute little blonde on the 8.31 from Sydenham to Charing Cross. I was the guy in the orange T shirt who couldn't take his eyes off you. Drink?'

I glanced up from the personal ads in the freebie press. She was seated almost opposite, and we held each other's gaze for perhaps the longest three seconds in our lives. We pressed every button, rang every bell.

That included our pride, our diffidence, our dignity, whatever you liked to call it. We weren't the types to push ourselves forward or to make the first move. We waited for others to come to us. And we could be easily hurt.

So there we sat, under the sanitised white light of the compartment, not daring to raise our eyes again.

Goodge Street, Tottenham Court Road, Leicester Square, and the longer we did nothing the worse it got.

Embankment, and back into the tunnel one more time, now beneath the river and the stanchions of Hungerford Bridge that carried the cute little blonde and her ogling admirer on the 8.31 from Sydenham into Charing Cross.

Waterloo. With a sudden convulsive effort she jumped up first and stood by the doors with her back half to me. God, if I'd reached out and touched her we'd have blown every fuse from High Barnet to Morden.

Down onto the platform, a little way behind her, then up the steps, along the corridor, onto the escalator. Time was fast running out.

'To the lady in the grey trouser suit on the Northern Line......'

* * * * *

43

BLACK COFFEE

I'd hardly given graphology a thought until I met Edith at a party. She was an expert on handwriting, and she pricked up her ears when I told her I was left-handed. Sinister types interested her.

Poring over my writing with her magnifying glass, she was especially struck by those large, pendulous loops that I sometimes executed. They were, she said, like cocoons, containing the chrysalis of a wild imagination. Release that and I might go far.

I reckoned I'd gone far enough, as her guest at this international seminar on handwriting, where my loops caused quite a stir.

'Went well, I thought,' Edith said, as we took a break at Tonopah Joe's Truck Stop, on the long hot drive back to the airport.

Through his windows I spotted a curious heap of rocks, sculpted and polished by sand and wind for a million years and presently roasting under the noonday sun like giant coffee beans.

I turned back to Tonopah Joe himself, seated by the old cash register. From his outsize baseball cap, pale moon face and five o'clock shadow, to his tartan shorts and bandy legs, he was made to sit on a ventriloquist's lap.

Or he was a Nibelung, one of that race of captive dwarfs in Wagner's 'Ring Cycle', who'd escaped to the Wild West, where he now crept out each night under the stars to quarry those wonderful coffee beans.

'A penny for your thoughts,' Edith inquired with a smile.

'Oh nothing,' I replied.

She blew on the piping hot brew in her cup. 'Good coffee,' she added.

'The best,' I agreed.

* * * * *

PAPER TIGER

Tippoo's Tiger was a great title for Richard's book. He'd taken it from an exhibit in the Victoria and Albert Museum, of a rotund and gaily painted tiger that growled as it savaged a red-coated soldier.

This mechanical wonder had once belonged to the Sultan Tippoo of Mysore, who led his armies against the British in India and was killed in battle in 1799.

It had also inspired Richard, with his interest in military history, to write an account of the Sultan's life and times. I'd watched him go bald and myopic as the piles of correspondence, the books and papers, pictures and maps, the stacks of typescript, grew ever higher.

And he wasn't finished yet. 'I must get out there,' he said. To India.

That left Blow Job, the novel he'd knocked out one wet weekend. He was going to take that to Hollywood. It was also his big chance to break into pictures, get back into acting.

Up on Richard's wall was an old poster for a production of King Lear, with his name among the cast. One or two others in that cast list were now household names of stage and screen. It hadn't happened for him.

Three years at RADA. Nothing from his bloody agent since Christ knows when. It made him sick.

Richard blinked through his glasses and his window at a floodlit Tower Bridge. There were thousands out there who'd pay a small fortune for that view. He was behind with the rent.

'I mean.' He reached for my bottle on the floor, where the lino curled up at the edges. 'What have I got to lose?'

Not his hair, I thought, balancing a plate of spaghetti on my knee.

* * * * *

OLD PAL

Debbie and I bobbed up and down with each passing wave before it broke with a sigh upon the shore.

Debbie had organised the holiday. A pity she had to drag Miriam along. There she sat, back on the beach, in her spot of shade, chubby legs stuck out from under her cotton dress, red where the sun had briefly touched them. She couldn't swim, and anyway she'd be too scared of the sharks and the jellyfish. How different could two sisters be?

At least Miriam had found a friend in Pal. I came out of the water and he sat up and licked his balls. With his long snout and pointed ears he made me think of Anubis, the sacred jackal of Egyptian mythology. But we called him Pal on account of the tins of dog food Miriam bought for him, together with a bowl. He'd filled out nicely in the last few days.

Debbie tripped over Pal, reaching for her towel. 'Better say goodbye to him now,' she said rather sharply to her sister. 'There won't be time in the morning.' I'd clean forgotten. We were off again tomorrow.

Debbie gathered her things and marched up the beach, swinging her delectable hips.

Miriam clung to Pal. 'Come on,' I said, gently releasing her hands and arms. 'Easy does it,' I gasped, taking her weight up the loose and shifting sand.

Behind us Pal was settling down again on the beach, next to his bowl. He'd be waiting in the morning.

There was a moment when the temperature dipped, before the hot blanket of night came down.

'He'll be all right,' I whispered to Miriam, wiping sweat from my eyes. At that moment I think I loved her.

* * * * *

YULE TIDE

The sea was calm, the tide was out, and gulls flapped and squabbled and stirred up the water in a large rock pool before settling for the night, at not much after half past three in the afternoon. They didn't know or care what day it was.

Back in the car park we were reminded soon enough. Fairy lights from a score of Christmas trees winked and blinked with a clockwork apathy.

'Think of them in there,' I said to Jennie. 'Hot, exhausted, bloated, hungover, a row in the kitchen, the kids in tears, the Queen on the telly.'

I fiddled with the car keys. 'Weeks beforehand, everybody's running around like headless chickens, then before you can say Jingle Bells there's nothing left but the washing up. The more you expect the less you get.'

We turned back onto the road that switch-backed along the top of the chalk white cliffs. One good thing, we had that to ourselves.

'Spend, spend, spend, buy, buy, buy, like a plague of locusts. And it never ends. By this time they'll be sitting there fart-less, gaping at pictures of sand and sun and being told to book their summer holidays. Madness.'

Half way up the next incline the engine suddenly coughed, spluttered and died. I wrenched on the hand brake, tried the ignition a couple of times.

In the heavy silence Jennie pointed to the fuel gauge. Empty. She took in a deep breath. 'Talk, talk, talk. Now look at us.'

A first gust of wind and rain lashed the windscreen from out of the darkness.

'Well.' She turned on me a look of withering scorn. 'And where are we going for *our* fucking summer holiday?'

* * * * *

VIA CRUCIS

As David was a man of the church I thought he and his wife Jessica might be interested in my favourite local cemetery, so different from the ones they were used to at home.

We gazed over a low wall and across the valley to a ridge of stone and scrub crowned with outcrops of limestone, like dragons' teeth.

'Pity about the mistral,' I shouted, of the wind that was also a local speciality.

Tall dark cypresses, grown old and ample on the compost of death, sighed and creaked with each fierce, chill, bone-dry gust.

Jessica tugged at her shawl. 'Can we move on?'

The chapel was what I really wanted them to see. Its heavy oak door slammed shut behind us, and the sudden silence was awesome. A few wooden benches were drawn up before the bare white marble altar, while the light from one small east window fell like a tear upon the flagstones. We breathed in the smell of cold stone.

Jessica drew her shawl closer about her. 'This place,' she said, 'gives me the creeps.'

One more thing I wanted to show them before they went on their way. The large wrought iron crucifix that hung from my wall, stark and monastic.

'I found it chucked out on the cemetery dump. To tell the truth, sometimes at night I feel a sudden chill in the air, as though an unquiet spirit had come round here looking for it.'

Jessica drained her wine glass. 'David, it's time we made a move.'

She stuck her head out of their car window. 'We'll pray for you,' she cried, as the mistral blew them away.

* * * * *

PUNCH DRUNK

Rita sat Mr Punch on the arm of her sofa, red pugnacious face at one end, spindly legs at the other, and not much in between till someone stuck a hand up his backside.

'How'd you get mixed up in all this?' she asked me.

I explained that I was writing a book about Punch and Judy, saw Sam's show, met him a few times over a pint and learnt about such interesting things as his swazzle, an item he stuck in his mouth to get the squeaky rasping voice. Then he said he had to leave town for a while and asked if I could let Rita have his puppets for safekeeping. She lived out Essex way. And there I was.

Rita left a crimson smear of lipstick on her cigarette before she next picked up the Hangman, clutching a little string noose in his hand.

'Watch.' With a twist and a tug she pulled off his head.

'Well I never!' she exclaimed, in what sounded more like delight than surprise. Stuffed into the neck was a wad of banknotes. She raised her glass. 'Here's to old Sam!'

'Sam,' I echoed, spilling gin on the sofa.

In the morning I blinked through curtains strung like washing on a line, at the flat, desolate expanse of mud, weeds and broken tarmac I'd inched over in yesterday's fog.

'I know what this place was,' I cried. 'An air force base.'

'Well.' Rita, in dressing gown and fluffy pink slippers, handed me a mug of tea. 'It ain't bleedin' Leicester Square.'

At the door of the old control tower she came up close.

'For services rendered,' she breathed, and tucked a banknote down my shirt front. 'Come again some time.'

* * * * *

STILL LIFE

Carol yawned again, the flush of last night's wine still on her face.

'I dreamed of those sparrows,' she said as we breezed along, chasing the same grey-blue line of hills, mile after mile.

She spoke of the ones we'd seen in the romanesque abbey at Vézelay, chirping and flitting about the nave. We didn't expect to see birds inside a church in our squeaky clean world. But what could be more natural than God's creatures in God's house, the commonplace and the numinous made one?

You could say the same of those pilgrims gathered at Vézelay a thousand years ago, at the start of the long, long march to the shrine at Santiago de Compostela. A noisy, scruffy crowd, suddenly transformed by the clamour of the bells high above their heads and by the wide-eyed stone face of the risen Christ at the entrance to that marvellous nave.

'We've taken all the wonder out of life,' I said to Carol, just as the line of hills loomed up like a wave, then parted, to reveal our first vineyard, the rows of vines immaculately staked out, young shoots aflame, calling down the sun.

'Oh!' That made her sit up.

We turned a corner, and sprawled over the road was the freshly mangled body of a fox or hare.

'Oh God!' Carol buried her face in her hands and stayed that way.

She'd had a lousy time, with a messy divorce and trying to bring up a delinquent daughter on her own. Then I'd got her into bed and wished I hadn't. She deserved a break.

'Come on,' I said. 'Snap out of it.'

'Just shut up, please.'

'I'm sorry.'

* * * * *

CHILLED OUT

Roberta emerged from the kitchen with a gust of steam and a strong whiff of Brussels sprouts.

'Has everybody got a drink?' she asked, attempting a note of jollity. 'Adam, what are you drinking?'

'Bacardi and Coke, Mum.'

Roberta had a way of speaking, hesitant, querulous, and with a note of censure, that got right up some people's noses.

'Why,' she now asked him in just that tone of voice, 'do you always have to be different? What's wrong with sherry?'

The rest of us held our breath.

'Here we go again!' Adam crashed his glass down on a table, spilling the contents, stormed out of the room and straight out of the house, slamming the front door behind him. It was the same every year.

I waited a couple more minutes. 'Time I was off,' I said, finishing my glass, and left with rather less commotion.

What bliss to stretch the limbs, take in some air, escape from the Brussels sprouts, and be on the outside looking in.

The deepening murk of afternoon threw into relief other interiors, with fairy lights and Christmas trees, and people chatting, laughing, hugging, in an orgy of goodwill.

One brightly lit room was more like a stage set or tableau. A large dining table was abandoned to the dirty plates and dishes, nutshells, orange peel, spent crackers, and old Grandad, fallen forward in his chair, still with his paper hat on, fast asleep face down in his Christmas pudding and custard.

Someone in an open neck shirt, hands thrust deep into his trouser pockets for warmth, joined me in contemplation of the scene.

I turned to Adam. 'Says it all, really.'

* * * * *

CANDY FLOSS

Whoever said that it was better to travel hopefully than to arrive was bang on.

At the end of a drive across mountain and desert and down endless six-lane highways, we parked by a fringe of grubby sand and an overflowing trash can. A blackened jetty tumbled into the sea, and beyond that a small Ferris wheel reluctantly turned.

They had a better one on the old Palace Pier. They also had dodgem cars and a ghost train, beer and fish and chips, and candy floss, the gossamer white threads gathering magically round the stick into a pink fluffy ball that tasted of strawberry and sugar and melted back into nothing on the tongue. Life in a nutshell, or on a stick.

'Are you deaf?' Connie was shouting through cupped hands. 'Time to kill you said!'

That was before she ran off in search of a loo an hour and a half ago.

She tapped furiously at her watch. 'Well, I reckon we've got twenty-four hours of it now!'

We paused to watch an aircraft climb over the ocean, turn and head back towards the land. Other aircraft had done the same, but there was something about that one.

'I *knew* we should have gone straight back and checked in.' Connie's voice began to break. 'I *swear* this is the last time I go anywhere with you!'

Amen to that. Lights began to twinkle up the hill towards Sunset Boulevard, and my rolled-up trousers were getting wet.

Connie skipped back as the next little wave licked a few more inches up the sand.

'Are you going to stay out there all night?'

Just now we had all this time to kill.

* * * * *

NIGHT WATCH

When I climbed the stairs there were heaps of dead wasps on the bedroom floor, like the fallen in battle, and a faint smell of death hung in the hot and airless room.

Others still buzzed and wandered up and down the window panes, till they dropped in their turn.

In the silence of the house a ceaseless rustling and nibbling also reached my ears. It came from above the ceiling, in the corner, over by the wall. I'd never heard that sound before, but it didn't take long to guess what it was. A wasps' nest in the roof.

I'd always quite liked wasps, with their gaily striped bodies, long slender wings, little nodding heads, their taste for jam and honey, and they didn't sting if you left them alone.

A point to reflect upon as I lay prostrate upon the bed, nauseous and feverish, pulse racing madly, face and hands the colour of strawberry jam from all those stings. Trying to shove a piece of paper into the crack in the ceiling, where they were dropping down into the room from their nest, wasn't leaving them alone.

They weren't there by accident, of course. I'd loved that house and communed with it for so many years, filled it with books and paintings, and with the incense of wood smoke that lingered through each winter and greeted me each spring.

Now I was selling the place, I had betrayed its trust, and it had summoned those wasps to drive me out or kill me first.

I lay in the dark and listened to that diabolical rustling and nibbling, felt very afraid, and prayed for the night to end.

Remember this. We don't haunt places. They haunt us.

* * * * *

TIBBET'S RIDE

Frau Goering, as I called her, had a head like a medicine ball and the torso of a tank. She wore a brown-belted raincoat, woollen stockings and brogues, and marched along half way towards a goose-step. Worst of all was the mirthless smile. She must have suffered some trauma. She also scared me shitless.

Happily she was also a creature of habit, taking the same walk each day, up the Hill towards the Heath, where she turned right at the Green Man. Following at a safe distance, that left the coast clear for me to continue on my own walk, along the side of the Heath to Tibbet's Corner.

A gallows once stood there, from which Mr Tibbet, highwayman and footpad, swung by his neck. Or did he? I could find no trace of such a person in the local archives, going back three hundred years. Who cared? He fitted the bill.

Hallowed by time as well. A thief and a murderer, in fact or in legend, Mr Tibbet was fondly remembered by two place names and a monument. There he was in profile, frock coat and tricorne hat, crouching stealthily, flintlock in hand, raised high above the circling traffic, and daffodils at his feet.

He wouldn't know Tibbet's Ride today. But, God help me, I knew the figure crossing the dual carriageway by the lights and coming my way. The brown-belted raincoat, thick woollen stockings and brogues.

They never managed to hang Reichsmarschall Goering, but they might still try with her, if they could find a strong enough rope.

* * * * *

LAUGHING SAL

From the basement of Cliff House Diana stared through salt-caked windows at the hump of Seal Rock.

She turned back to the clutter of old pin-ball tables, baseball games, a fortune teller with her crystal ball, miniature cranes dangling over heaps of tarnished trinkets and charms, the graveyard of a penny arcade.

'Cheer up,' I said. 'Watch this.'

I inserted a dime into the glass case containing a small fairground organ or calliope. A perforated roll began jerkily to turn, bellows wheezed, clusters of rubber tubes, like veins and arteries, swelled and writhed, and there came a sudden blast of The Stars And Stripes Forever. Drums and cymbals joined in.

'Sousa!' I cried, beating time.

Diana clapped her hands to her ears.

That was something Laughing Sal couldn't do. She was a near life-size limbless torso, dressed in a polka dot red and white smock. She had a ginger wig and a shiny face with a grin that promised blue murder.

Another dime and Sal began to shudder and shake inside her own glass box, and to laugh and scream like someone laughing and screaming into a large empty jar. You could be drowning out there, reaching for a grip on the guano white sides of Seal Rock, the water heaving and sucking you down, while Sal went on laughing fit to bust.

'It's always what *you* want to do!' Diana sobbed. 'Call this a fucking holiday!'

Sal had suddenly gone very quiet, but kept on grinning.

Who's Got The Last Laugh Now. George and Ira Gershwin, I believe.

* * * * *

MISTER BIG

Conrad stood tall beneath his fancy black fedora and behind his dark glasses. He hailed a taxi to take us to our next working lunch.

Conrad was at his best checking columns of figures, drawing up schedules, directing operations like a general. And I was his lieutenant, drafting specimen texts, selecting pictures, getting things moving on the ground.

He'd said we were going to set the publishing world alight with our mail order series on The World of Opera, till it all went belly up. Cash flow problems, Conrad explained.

He assured me it wasn't going to happen with The Great Composers.

'The money's up front, we've got the American market tied up, and the translation rights, and we're already ninety per cent subscribed.'

Conrad spoke softly but urgently. He could sell snow to the Eskimos. 'This time,' he promised me, 'there'll be more work than you can shake a fist at!'

He settled back in the taxi. 'Tchaikovsky was queer, wasn't he?'

'Yes,' I replied, 'and his marriage was a disaster.'

Oh dear. Conrad had been through more marriages than I could shake a fist at. And the latest one, I gathered, was on the rocks.

The dark glasses gave nothing away, but he muttered something to the effect that, 'It's always the little things.'

At the restaurant he removed the fedora from his shining pate. Bald men had a certain reputation, after all.

At our table he lowered the glasses just enough to scan the wine list, with one good eye and one black one.

One of those little things, I supposed, as we settled for the Nuits-St-Georges.

* * * * *

DINNER DATE

Fred prised the lid off a fresh bucket of emulsion paint, and bang, I was back.

Fan blades languidly stirred the same spicy sweetness round the hotel lobby, dim and cool against the heat and glare of the day. Beyond was the large old colonial dining room, doors and shutters always open to the boom of surf at lunch time, to the blood-red sun as it spilled once more into an oil-calm sea.

Time for me to get back behind the baby grand, while small turbaned waiters put the finishing touches to the dinner tables.

Two evenings I'd sat there playing Over the Rainbow on sweaty keys, watching her watching me across the floor.

I'd previously spotted her down by the pool, under a shade, reading a book, quite happy to be on her own. She was no spring chicken, but she'd kept a figure that said she still had something to give.

Now at dinner, one of a jolly party, hair brushed back over her ears, and in a silvery dress that shimmered as she moved, she nodded and laughed on cue, while her eyes kept wandering elsewhere.

Her husband, it had to be, dispatched the waiter with a gin and tonic for the pianist. I nodded and smiled my thanks, and she didn't know where to look.

Our rainbow ended and they all got up to go. One last quick glance over her lightly tanned shoulder for us both to remember. Too bad, we tacitly agreed, that's life.

Fred put the lid firmly back on his bucket of paint. He noticed my piano.

'Play much?' he asked.

'Used to,' I said.

* * * * *

LAST RITES

We must have joined this procession of big black limousines as they came through the cemetery gates. Easily done in the pouring rain. Anyway, there we were stuck in the middle of them, being shunted back to what was presumably the home of the deceased.

Still trapped there, nose to tail, we watched them all hurry up the steps to the glass fantail over the front door and out of the rain.

'Listen,' I said to Jill. 'We're lost, we've missed our crossing, and I reckon they owe us a drink.' I reached for jacket and tie. 'Come on. With that crowd they'll never notice us.'

A maid greeted us with liqueur glasses on a silver tray. Cognac, Armagnac, it hit the spot.

'You know,' I said to Jill, 'they should do a Michelin Guide to some of these cemeteries. Crosses for interest, skulls for atmosphere.'

There were also tables laden with food and wine.

'The funeral baked meats did coldly furnish forth the marriage table.' I smacked my lips. 'Hamlet.'

'Alas poor Yorick.' Jill waved her glass. 'Like your Michelin thing. Yorick and his skulls.'

'Keep your voice down.' I handed her a plate and fork. 'Better eat something.'

'A funeral baked bean?' Jill collapsed with laughter on the edge of a trestle table and down she went, with a bowl of mayonnaise.

In a soaking drizzle I sprinted for our little car, now on its own.

'Wait!' Jill wailed. 'I think I'm going to be sick.'

She was. At the top of a flight of steps, under a glass fantail, with a lot of mayonnaise.

* * * * *

RED ALERT

Herpes Zoster is not the name of an ancient fire god, it's shingles. But it feels like fire, the pain that burns its way right down to the bone.

'Oh, you poor boy!' Rosalind cried. Her old dad had shingles in the face and lost the sight of one eye. Well, I had it round the crutch, and we'd have to wait and see what I might lose the use of.

'You should be home in bed,' she added. I know, but she wasn't there to tuck me in, which is why I came to their offices with my next lot of text on disk, just to see her again.

Her phone buzzed angrily. Rosalind jumped up as though she'd been stung. Toby always had first call.

A black bear of a man, soaked in aftershave and deodorant and stripped down to those scarlet braces, dyed in the blood and guts of his minions. He'd bawled and bullied to build up his business, selling mail order books, magazines and records, and he didn't know how to stop. Listen to him now.

Rosalind came rushing out of his office again, and she couldn't hide the tears. The shame, the humiliation, dinner one night each week, the hotel room afterwards, then to yell at her like that, so that everyone in the office could hear, and half the street as well.

She called the airline, to cancel one flight and book another. Toby and his wife, off to New York for a week. She finished and made a big thing of blowing her nose.

'We're a fine pair, aren't we!' She sniffed and tried a brave little smile, smoothing away some of the tiredness round eyes and mouth.

Yes, and why couldn't we have had a go. At least I'd still be there when she woke up.

* * * * *

75

FRENCH KISS

Gordon's way of learning French was to read Proust with the aid of a very fat dictionary. It didn't help when he went round the shops. He pointed mutely at what he wanted, paid each time with a fresh note because that was easier, grabbed the change, and fled.

Why had someone so timid and tongue-tied moved abroad and to our village in the first place? Gordon told me it was to get away from it all and write a book. Bald and bewhiskered, he looked a bit like Tolstoy, if that helped any.

'Is it a novel?' I asked.

Gordon had said more than enough, and rather desperately changed the subject. 'The girl in the baker's shop is rather nice,' he muttered.

'Actually,' I replied, 'she's been asking about you.'

He turned a beetroot red beneath his whiskers, swilled the wine faster round his glass, sniffed it, and stammered, 'I fear it is still a little t-too young.'

Speaking of age, girl was stretching it a bit. She'd been around, and maybe it was handling those baguettes, still warm from the oven, that turned her on.

I loved the way she said 'au revoir', catching at her breath and tickling her epiglottis with the tip of her tongue. I wished she'd tickle mine.

I asked Gordon, 'Shall I give her your love?'

We won't see him in the boulangerie again, not until he's finished Proust or his novel, whichever is the soonest.

Meantime, I'll buy his bread and croissants for him, help him shift some of that small change, and wave my baguette each time the lady says, 'au revoir'.

* * * * *

LOST LADY

'Excuse me.' This old lady sat on a low garden wall. She was decently dressed, with her shopping bag beside her. The voice was as fragile as the rest of her. 'But do you know the name of this road? You see, I can't remember where I live.'

It's not every day you meet someone who's just lost a part of their mind. It was a shock.

'Do you recognise any of this?' I waved an arm about me, at the road, the blocks of flats, the trees and shrubs.

She shook her head. Then she raised a thin, blue-veined hand against the sun. 'I say, just behind you, isn't that a beautiful rose!'

The creamy white bloom was tinged with crimson, a floral menstruation.

'Yes,' I agreed, 'and just down the road there's a lovely big clump of lavender. It's in flower right now and I love watching the bumble bees buzzing and bobbing from flower to flower.'

'I can see,' the old lady said, 'that you haven't lost a sense of wonder. You still have time to stand and stare. You must be a very happy man.'

I shook my head in turn. 'The trouble is that the more aware, the more sensitive you are to everything around you, the more you can get hurt. I sometimes wish I had no feelings at all.'

The other smiled sweetly. 'All the same, talking to you has made me feel so much better!'

I smiled back. 'Me too!'

That was the trouble with conversations. You soon forgot what started them.

* * * * *

BABY FACE

'Could you take Baby for a walk,' Beth asked, as she started mopping up in the car. A bit late for that, I thought.

Beth was a pet therapist, but she couldn't use Baby any more. Leave him alone with anyone for five minutes and they'd be ready to jump off the Brooklyn Bridge. Those frantic dashes among the piss-stained trash cans and hydrants up and down East Tenth Street had nearly done for me.

Still, now that we'd arrived, Chestnut Avenue, in view of the Catskill Mountains, looked a happier prospect, and that bend in the road where it dipped among tall trees beckoned me on.

Deep in their shade, the old clapboard house stared back through empty windows. Perhaps it had seen a murder, or perhaps a black hole from outer space had landed and sucked the light and life right out of it.

Could I yet hear the ghostly chime of the grandfather clock that stood by the dark mahogany stairs? The creak of a floorboard up in the lonely turret room, where the piebald rocking horse still tipped gently to and fro at the touch of an unseen hand?

Baby had also gone very quiet, crouched by the side of the road and trying something more ambitious. Let him leave his calling card among those overgrown bushes by the porch with the broken swing, and see if he disappeared up his own black hole.

He finished and looked hopefully up at me. We all need to be loved, especially superannuated off-white poodles with bad kidneys and bad breath.

'Come on, for God's sake.' I tugged at his lead before anyone else saw what we'd done.

* * * * *

BON VOYAGE

Sid and Edna stepped off the train looking like they'd landed on Mars.

'Bit different from Lewisham,' I said cheerily, as we drove back into the hills at sundown with the scent of thyme blowing in through the car window. They had nothing to say.

They hardly made a sound till next morning, when I heard Edna's voice from the room upstairs. She hadn't slept a wink, what with the noise of all those bloody frogs, and bitten all over.

'Fat lot you care,' she went on. 'Go on, finish the bottle. My mother was right about you.'

'Your mother,' Sid replied, picking his words, 'was a miserable nosy old bag.'

That did it. Violence in real life, even a little domestic ding dong, isn't anything like the choreographed antics we see on screen. It's clumsy, helpless and despairing, just the sound of it, and the loaded silence afterwards, of shame and guilt, is even worse.

An hour later they knocked on my door. Edna had on a pair of dark glasses, Sid wore a plaster on his chin. They'd packed and they were off again, and they wouldn't let me drive them back to the station.

So I left them at the bus stop, waiting in what little shade there was, the big brown suitcase between them.

Their daughter had rented the small apartment in my house, to give mum and dad a special holiday for their silver wedding. I dare say she pictured some little white villa nestling among the pines with a path down to the sea.

Not, I suspect, that it would have made much difference.

* * * * *

CREEPY CRAWLIES

Open day at the Insect House, and Kate our hostess reminded us, 'Spiders aren't really insects, they're arachnids. They have eight legs. But we're one big happy family in here!'

So saying she reached into a glass tank and brought out Judy from Trinidad.

'Don't the females eat their mates?' asked a youth with acne and a squint.

'Sometimes Derek.' Kate evidently knew him as a regular visitor. She stroked Judy's walnut-sized abdomen as much as to say, don't listen to the nasty man, and Judy daintily curled up her legs, a bit like somebody's fingers.

So what was this stomach-churning, heart-stopping arachnophobia, lodged deep in the collective unconscious? It had to come from somewhere. Not perhaps from the tiny money spider with her promise of good luck. The kind you sometimes found in the bath was more like it. Bloated grey bellies suspended between eight long bristly legs, and a manic turn of speed. The cocoons they spun around points of light, to lure to their doom other hapless creatures with tiny wings. Motionless they waited, pinhead eyes unblinking, till the moment came to pounce and bite and paralyse and gorge.

Derek scratched at a pimple. 'Put her in with a scorpion.'

Kate ignored him and returned Judy to her own tropic enclave, where she crawled under a piece of bark and curled back into a fluffy ball.

Tomorrow more young faces pressed against the glass, eager to be chilled and thrilled by something so damnably hard to spot.

'Look, there it is!'

Yes, and look who's right behind you, with his own cross-eyed view of life. How many legs could Derek count on Judy? Sixteen? Try him with a millipede.

* * * * *

JUMBO JET

Sarah banged on my door. 'Wake up lazy bones!' She was a nurse and she didn't believe in jet lag. 'Hurry up, or you'll miss the bus!'

She saved me a seat on the one that took us to the temple of Wat Po. I gazed at inscrutable words of wisdom inscribed on the great flat feet of the reclining Buddha, while Sarah stood by his serene and golden head.

'Come on, slow coach!' she beckoned with a smile.

After lunch they were off again to the Floating Market, or somewhere. I needed a kip.

A brazen hoot woke me this time. Down in the street a small bow-legged man in dhoti and turban brandished a curved brass horn. Behind him came an elephant, trunk swinging idly to his shambling gait. No buns for him, no gorgeous silks for the parade. Across his neck was a plain wooden box, half filled with junk. A second hoot and man and elephant turned the hot and dusty corner and were gone.

'Hey!' I greeted Sarah at supper time. She was starting to tan, and that diaphanous dress did her no harm either. 'You'll never guess what I saw!'

She smiled again and sat down with this other guy. She was still with him as we headed home, chasing the veil of night across two continents at thirty thousand feet, our lives on hold.

I waited by the luggage carousel under the cold neon light of a colder dawn. Two bags, his and hers, came round together.

Sarah turned and waved. 'Have fun!'

* * * * *

FAG END

Cyril's head and face were like a head hunter's trophy, the grey shrunken features, the scraps of stubble and hair, the skull-like rictus of a grin.

That's what forty fags a day for forty years had done for him. They'd also kippered and cured him and preserved him from all infection. He never caught a cold and never missed a party. As tenacious as a flea as well if he got hold of you. Take evasive action, fast.

'Hi there!' I tucked myself in next to Anthea, over by the door. Her face was no oil painting, but the rest of her I fancied something rotten.

I pointed to her glass. 'Can I top you up?'

Toying with his next cigarette, Cyril bobbed up between us.

'Have you seen anything of Joan lately?' he asked me in his gas pipe voice.

Always the same bloody question, always when I was with another woman.

'No I haven't.' I looked round and Anthea had gone. I pushed past him. 'Excuse me, I'm off.'

Outside in the bleak courtyard, I could at least breathe again. I stepped over the fragments of a broken bottle, glistening under the light of a street lamp, waiting for the next hapless drunk to trip and fall, and jumped thankfully aboard a bus.

So did Cyril. He flashed his freedom pass, sat down beside me and fiddled with his hearing aid. 'How far are you going?' he asked.

All the way with Anthea, given half a bleedin' chance.

* * * * *

LITTLE OTTO

'I *do wish* you wouldn't call me that!' Elizabeth protested as we drove past fields of sugar cane, cows munching at their fringes with a bovine indifference to heat.

'Sorry darling,' Sylvia replied as usual, and winked at me in the driving mirror.

The two of them ran a small arty magazine and they'd published one or two of my pieces. They also found me a useful male to make up the numbers at their dinner parties, and now to share the cost of a holiday in the sun, handle the luggage, and so forth.

Back on the beach, Elizabeth dug her sunshade into the sand and disappeared behind mammoth dark glasses and a book. Sylvia and I stripped down for a swim.

At the line of buoys marking the limit of safe bathing, she handed me her mask and snorkel, wet skin brushing wet skin, then bobbed under the water, blew a stream of it in my face, winked again, and headed back for the shore.

Looking down through the mask, a small object glided over the sun-flecked rocks. A baby octopus. He found a crevice and tucked himself in till you wouldn't know he was there. That's what you could do without any bones.

Elizabeth's trouble was too many bones. 'What a disgusting thing to do!' she shouted, as I raised my head from Little Otto's world to mine. 'Spitting water like that!'

'Lizzie darling,' Sylvia pleaded. 'It was just a bit of fun.'

'Fun!' Elizabeth choked on the word. She flung down her book, struggled to her feet and tried running up the beach in her flip flops. 'And I *do wish* you wouldn't call me that!'

* * * * *

HAPPY DAYS

'Like some?' Terry joined me on the seat with a bottle of bubbly, and together we watched the merry throng having their pictures taken.

'What a game, eh!' he said.

I wiped the neck of the bottle. 'Not your wedding, is it?'

'Not this time!' Terry loosened his collar and tie and stretched out his legs. 'Still, nice place for it.'

The big Gothic house was dressed in stucco as white as the icing on a wedding cake. Beyond the sweep of lawn and the rose garden were the rolling acres of park land where they were making hay, and not another building in sight.

He lit up. 'You been married?'

'Divorced.' You can sometimes speak more freely with a stranger than with a friend. 'That's the easy part. It's afterwards, waking up in the night and going over it all again, the shame, the guilt and the regrets.' I took another swig. 'Mind you, love affairs can be worse. You can't win.'

'Terry!' A young woman in a floral hat and gripping a large shiny black handbag stood a little way down the path.

'Where've you been!' She glared accusingly at me and the bottle and beckoned impatiently at him. 'Come on, it's goin' to pour in a minute!'

The sky had turned the colour of a deep bruise. There was a flicker and a rumble over towards Epsom Downs, and that rare and transient fragrance as the first swollen raindrops soaked into warm, dry ground.

Terry straightened his collar and tie, adjusted the white carnation in his button hole, clambered to his feet, crushed out his cigarette.

'What a game, eh!'

* * * * *

SOUTHERN BELLE

Mardi Gras. Fat Tuesday. And bloody cold on Wednesday. A few shrivelled balloons still lolled from balconies, and in Jackson Square a lone black man blew a few tuneless notes on a sousaphone before he stopped to blow on his hands. It was warmer on the bus.

'It's hot in here!' this old woman suddenly bawled from the back seats.

The driver glanced nervously in his mirror as we pulled out of the depot. He needn't have worried, we soon got used to her mad outbursts. Indeed, she entertained us, until the mind began to slip its gears to the endless smack and spin of vulcanised rubber on road and long day slipped into night.

'I'm diabetic,' she announced, when we stopped for coffee and donuts at Atlanta at some ungodly hour.

'What's that say?' she demanded, waking us to stiff necks and pins and needles. It was a road sign to the battlefields of Fredericksburg and Spotsylvania. The Civil War, and Confederate territory. We still had a long way to go.

'Where are we now?' she cried, as we crossed the Potomac and Capitol Hill rose in a high tide of light. The last five minutes of thirty-one hours on the road.

Off the bus and for the first time I got a good look at her. A tiny figure for such a voice, she squatted on a portable stool in an oily puddle by the empty baggage hold. Big wet snowflakes drifted out of the darkness, settling on her iron grey hair or sliding down her torn black plastic mac.

'Where's my valise?' she asked me, all the wind and piss gone out of her.

On A Streetcar Named Desire.

* * * * *

COPY CAT

Van Gogh's Sunflowers was propped against the television in the living room of Oliver's council flat.

'That's new,' I said, looking for somewhere to sit, on a chair or on the floor.

Now retired, Oliver was a frustrated artist who made copies of famous paintings that were probably good enough to get him into trouble if he tried to sell them. So you had to get past the Mona Lisa at the front door, and in the bathroom you took a piss with The Laughing Cavalier.

'Yes,' he said of Sunflowers. 'Look at Van Gogh's amazing eye for colour, yellow on yellow, and his use of impasto. You have to work the paints with your thumb.' He went through the motions in the air. 'The Fauves owed an awful lot to him. Matisse, Braque, Vlaminck, that crowd.'

'The wild beasts,' Pam interpolated, as she entered the living room sideways, juggling with three plates of sausage and mash.

Oliver balanced one of them on his lap. 'Now what the hell are you on about!'

Pam perched on the piano stool. 'That's what *fauves* means in French, dickhead. Wild beasts.'

Not how I'd describe Picasso, Pam's old black tom, a creature of stupendous girth.

'Watch that bloody cat!' Oliver caught hold of his plate just in time. 'The paint's still wet!'

'Tell you what,' I said to him. 'You should do Guernica next.'

'You're joking!' he spluttered through a mouthful of mashed potato. 'Have you seen the fucking size of it!'

I winked at Picasso. He blinked at me.

* * * * *

MONKEY NUTS

Who'd have thought there'd be so many morbid types, queueing up for the trip to see a Hindu cremation. Anyway, I was too late. That left the other trip, to some lousy ruined temple with the sacred monkeys.

I sat on the bus and sulked, till I noticed this woman, a few rows up, who kept tossing her hair to steal another half glance at me, the mystery man behind his silver-tinted glasses. You can tell.

We drew up by a vertiginous line of cliffs that could almost have been Brittany or Cornwall, the cliffs, the wind, the foaming sea.

Tristan and Isolde. I heard again those desolate chords, rising up on the strings of the orchestra and dissolving into thin air, as the mortally wounded Tristan lay among those ruins, waiting for the first sight on the empty line of the horizon of a sail, of Isolde's returning ship.

Hang on. Australia was somewhere over that shark-infested ocean, and my Isolde, so to speak, was feeding the monkeys.

I took off the silver-tinted glasses to try and open my own packet of peanuts. A simian hand snatched them from me, scattering peanuts everywhere. A sacred sphincter disappeared behind a pile of stones.

'Talk about cheeky monkey!' she cried, so that everybody else from the bus could hear.

I bought a new pair of dark glasses to hide behind and a plastic eye piece fell out of them.

'Be seein' yer, Lord Nelson!' she bawled.

Yeah, from on top of the next funeral pyre. Hand me the kerosene.

* * * * *

JOLLY ROGER

Wendy invited me to the office Christmas lunch.

She'd arrived at Rainbow Publications as Roger's temp, and as quiet as a church mouse at first. Then she dropped the skirt and blouse for a trouser suit, and the contact lenses for horn-rimmed spectacles. His personal assistant now, with an office of her own.

At the restaurant she'd reserved a place for each of us, with our name on a card, plus a cracker to get us in the party mood.

Bang. A pink paper hat for me, and a joke. Help me doctor, I think I'm a pair of curtains. Pull yourself together, man.

Bang. A skull and crossbones for Roger, and a joke. Why don't owls make love in the rain? Wait for it. Because it's too wet to woo.

The restaurant filled up, it was hot, you couldn't hear yourself speak, and someone got the hiccups and the giggles. I waved at Roger, indicated my watch, and mouthed the words, 'Got to go'. From the head of the table Wendy, in jester's cap and bells, waved back.

Never mind the rain. I strode along to the Emperor Concerto. Not Beethoven's name for it, of course. Now I remembered why I wanted a quick word with Roger. Musical nicknames. Emperor Concerto, Moonlight Sonata, Raindrop Prelude. A nice little filler for the next edition of Classical Hits. A quick word with Roger. That's all it used to take. You needed a bloody passport to see him nowadays.

At Hammersmith Broadway a taxi pulled up at the lights, with a glimpse inside of a cap and bells and a skull and crossbones, somewhat askew.

The lights turned green. Where to now, guv? Wapping. Execution Dock.

* * * * *

BONNE NUIT

'In the Middle Ages,' I said, 'they'd have burnt Gustave as a witch.'

He had the face of a gargoyle and lived in a filthy old house down the hill from the village with a family of poor mangy cats who hung around the place like gruesome familiars.

The odd thing about those cats was that they never seemed to multiply. That, so it was whispered in the village, was because Gustave sometimes had one of them for supper. He spoke in grunts and squeaks, as though he had a piece of claw stuck in his throat. Not that he ever had much to say, all on his own down at the sewage plant in his blue overalls and black beret till the day he died.

'Listen!' Cathy sat by a corner of the hearth. 'It's stopped.'

The storm had rumbled on and an immense silence now filled the night outside. My friends began to stir.

'I'll just pop downstairs,' Cathy said.

With those big green eyes and that raven black hair perhaps she was a witch, who could change into a succubus and come to my bed as I slept to sate herself of my manhood.

'You're nearly out of soap,' she informed me, coming back up the stairs and pulling on her woolly cap.

I know, and it didn't matter. One last ember flickered and died among the ashes of the fire. Life ebbing from the old house for another year, soon to be shuttered and bolted through the long cold winter months.

Places can get just as lonely as people who knew how to skin a cat for the pot.

* * * * *

BOTTOMS UP

A hint of crème de menthe, I thought, taking another sip.

'Didn't cocktails begin with Prohibition?' I asked.

Right country, Jim replied, but they went back to at least 1809, when someone in Kentucky produced a mix of spirits, bitters and sugar that he called a cocktail.

Jim topped me up from his silver shaker. The name cocktail, he said, may have been taken from the local word for a bob-tailed horse. Or it may be derived from the name of an Aztec princess, Xochtitl, who was said to have invented an elixir of love. It was all in his book.

Aztec princess! Elixir of love! I couldn't wait to tell my editor, Fiona. She was one of the county set and neurotic as hell. Think of that painting by Edvard Munch, The Scream, the matchstick wrists and hands clutching the emaciated face, the mouth a little hole of panic and fear. That was her.

I grabbed Jim's phone. Let's have a word with The Scream!

'Fiona? It's me. Listen, my computer's crashed. All right, calm down. I'm at the repair shop now.' I glanced round at the clutter of computer offal on the work top, and at all the bottles in the sink. 'Jim's a computer wizard. He's also writing a book about cocktails. He's just invented a new one.'

I sighed heavily. 'Cocktails, Fiona. Right up your street. Manhattan, Bloody Mary, Screwdriver, Rusty Nail, Zombie, Harvey Wallbanger.'

'What? Wall, Fiona, as in bricks. Yes. Banger, as in sausage.'

The stupid bitch hung up. I looked round at Jim and held out my glass. 'See what I mean?'

* * * * *

POST SCRIPT

If you're in a hole stop digging. Good advice, but none of us likes to admit defeat. I went on scribbling a word in here, scratching one out there, getting nowhere but unable to stop.

A lousy day all round. The still tender and unsullied leaves on the trees outside my window shivered in the cold wind of late spring, learning the hard way fast. And a little way down the road was that car, with a stack of rain-soaked parking tickets shoved under the windscreen. An old family saloon, with tarnished paint work and spots of rust, it had crawled there to die.

I felt sorry for the car. I felt something else for the small fluffy striped tiger left on top of the dashboard, button eyes raised helplessly to the windscreen and those soggy parking tickets. He'd never had much going for him. He had nothing now. The bottom line was that I couldn't walk past that sad vehicle and its solitary occupant again. Every day I must go the long way round to the shops.

With all the willpower I could muster, I stopped what I was doing, screwed up another useless piece of paper into a ball, and stood up, cold and numb.

Why did I feel such heart-rending pity for inanimate objects, from abandoned cars to fluffy toys? There was another subject, another hole to start digging into. One day I might strike that pot of gold.

First things first. Down to the shops, the long way round. Bread, soup, fish fingers.

* * * * *